go girl

flip it!

Jackson's
Side

hardie grant EGMONT

Twin Trouble

by
Sally Rippin

Illustrations by
Aki Fukuoka

hardie grant EGMONT

Chapter One

'OK,' Jackson's mum called. 'Time to go!'

Jackson ran down the stairs towards the front door, his bag banging against his back. He was racing his twin sister to the car, but his bag felt so heavy with new books that it was slowing him down.

He knew he didn't have to take all his books to school on the first day. But he'd

been feeling nervous, so he'd shoved them all in.

In their old house, he would have asked Sienna which books to bring. She would've even helped him pack them into his bag so that they didn't stick into his back. But since they'd moved into their new house, they didn't share a room anymore. Sienna had been all the way down the end of the hall when he was packing his bag, singing loudly and happily in her own bedroom.

So many things were different now that the twins had moved to the city from the little country town where they'd grown up. But having different rooms was what felt the strangest for Jackson. *We've always shared a room*, he thought. *I really miss having her around all the time.*

He knew it was a bit babyish, but if he ever woke up with a nightmare or a worry at their old house, it was enough just to hear Sienna breathing in the dark to know that he was not alone.

I feel very sorry for people who aren't twins, he thought. *It must be so lonely. It's bad enough having Sienna all the way down the other end of the hall!*

Jackson ran as fast as he could, but Sienna had beaten him to the car again. Their mum followed behind, looking flustered. Jackson knew that this meant they were running late. It made him feel even more nervous.

'Sorry, kids, I lost track of the time!' their mum said, jangling the keys in her hand.

Jackson hated being late. He'd set his alarm clock for six o'clock especially so that he'd have plenty of time to be ready for his first day at the new school. He'd even laid his new school uniform out the night before.

Dad had been awake nice and early too, so he and Jackson had eaten breakfast together. Sienna and their mum had slept in, like they always did.

'I win *again*! You've got to speed up, little bro,' Sienna teased, poking her tongue out at him. 'Looks like I get the front seat again!'

Jackson just shrugged. He didn't care about winning as much as Sienna did. He just wanted to get to school on time.

'Come on, kids,' their mum said, unlocking the car. 'You can both hop in the back.'

Jackson opened the door and peered into the back seat. 'But all your canvasses are still in there!' he groaned.

'Oh, I forgot,' their mum said. 'Well, we haven't got time to get them out now. You can get in the front, Sienna. Jackson, just push that stuff onto the floor, love.'

It was always messy with his mum's art stuff. Old canvasses, paint tubes and brushes rolled around on the floor. You

never knew what would be sticking to you when you got out. Jackson checked the seat carefully before climbing in. He didn't want to get paint on his new uniform.

Sienna always said that she was allowed the front seat because she was the eldest, even though it was only by four minutes. Still, Jackson had to admit that it sometimes felt like she was much older. And even though he wished *he* could sit in the front seat occasionally, he loved that Sienna always looked after him like he was her little brother.

As they drove to their new school, there was only one thought that helped calm the butterflies in Jackson's stomach. *I'm so glad Sienna will be there to look after me today.*

Chapter Two

When they got to school, Sienna quickly disappeared into her new classroom. Jackson couldn't believe she was so relaxed about walking into a room of kids she didn't know!

He saw her talking to her new teacher, who was smiling and nodding at her. Jackson felt the knot in his tummy tighten. Then he felt his mum's hand rest gently on his shoulder and he turned to look up at her. She smiled and crouched down so that her face was on the same level as his.

'You'll be fine, darling,' she said softly.

Jackson swallowed hard. 'I don't feel well,' he said.

His mum cupped his face with her hand. Her hand felt nice and cool on his hot cheek. 'You really will be just fine,' she said.

'Why can't I be in the same class as Sienna?' he asked, as they walked towards his classroom. He scuffed a moon shape in the dry dirt with his shoe. He already knew the answer, but he couldn't help asking all the same.

His mum gave him a little smile. 'We've talked about this already, darling. It will be good for both of you.'

'But we've always been in the same class,' he said quietly.

'Your last school only had eighty-seven students, Jackson. There was only one class in your year level. The teachers here think it's good for twins to be separated, and I agree with them. You and Sienna have a great relationship, but it's good for you to develop as individuals, too.'

Jackson kept his eyes on the ground. 'But I like being with Sienna.'

'I know, love,' said his mum kindly. 'And she likes being with you. But she wants to make some new friends. And you'll make friends, too! You'll see.'

No, I won't, Jackson thought. *I'm too shy. Sienna's the one that makes friends easily.*

'Come on,' said his mum. 'Let's go and meet your new teacher. I'm sure he'll be lovely.'

She took his hand and led him towards his classroom. Jackson followed, but his stomach really *had* started to hurt. He wondered where the sick bay was.

'Here we are,' his mum said as they arrived at the doorway of a noisy classroom.

Jackson looked inside. There were so many kids! And they were all chatting loudly and wandering around the room. It was obvious that everyone knew each other, and knew what to do.

Jackson felt his mum's hand slip out of

his as she nudged him gently inside. He took a deep breath and stepped into the room. His legs had never felt so wobbly.

The teacher looked up as Jackson walked in. 'Ah, here's our new student!' he called cheerfully. 'Jackson, isn't it? We're glad you're here. I'm Mr Paul.'

Jackson turned around to look at his mum. She blew a kiss from behind the doorway, where no-one else could see her. Jackson liked the look of Mr Paul. He had the kind of face that looked ready to tell a good joke at any time.

Mr Paul put his hand out to Jackson and Jackson shook it. He felt very grown-up shaking hands.

'Luke!' Mr Paul bellowed to a boy at the back of the classroom. 'Clear a spot for Jackson to sit down, please. Luke is our resident clown, aren't you, Luke?'

'I try my best, Mr Paul,' Luke said with a grin.

'I'm sure that Luke will keep you entertained, Jackson,' said Mr Paul.

Jackson walked over to where Luke was and sat down at the desk next to him.

Luke had scruffy blond hair and freckles, and a big gap between his front teeth, which made his grin look even goofier. 'Hey!' he said.

'Hi,' said Jackson. He smiled shyly.

His tummy ache was already starting to feel a little better.

'Right,' said Mr Paul. 'Now if you'll all settle down we can get started. Our year level's project for this term is – The Environment. Our class will be looking at the effects of the drought, and ways we can save water. Does anyone have any suggestions?'

'We could drink cola instead of water,' said Luke under his breath.

Jackson grinned. He liked stupid jokes, even though Sienna thought they were silly. Without even thinking, he leant over to Jackson and whispered, 'What do frogs drink?'

Luke shrugged his shoulders.

'Croak-a-cola,' Jackson whispered with a grin.

Luke laughed loudly.

'Luke,' called Mr Paul, 'what's so funny? It would be great if you could share it with us.'

Jackson suddenly felt sick again. *What if Luke dobs me in?* he thought. *What if I get told off?* He couldn't believe he'd told a joke when they were meant to be listening to Mr Paul. He was definitely going to be in trouble in front of everyone. And Sienna wasn't there to stick up for him!

But then Luke said, 'Well, I was just thinking that we should all drink cola, instead of water!' He smiled at Jackson.

He didn't tell on me! Jackson thought, surprised.

'Not quite the brilliant answer I was looking for, Luke,' Mr Paul smiled. 'But good try. How about you, Jackson? What did you do in the country to save water?'

Jackson felt his cheeks burn. He didn't like answering questions in class. 'Well, we had a tank to collect rainwater to water the garden,' he said quietly.

'A water tank!' Mr Paul exclaimed. 'That's the kind of idea I'm looking for. Well done, Jackson.'

Jackson felt his cheeks get even hotter, but he felt happy.

'Why don't we get a water tank for school, then?' one of the girls suggested.

'Then we could water the footy oval so we can use it again!' Luke called out.

'Hand up, Luke,' said Mr Paul. 'Water tanks are expensive. And we would need a very big one to water an oval.'

'Well —' started Luke.

'Hand *up*, please, Luke,' repeated Mr Paul.

Luke shot his hand into the air. 'Can't we ask everybody to put some money in?' he suggested. 'Like all our parents?'

'It's not that easy, Luke,' Mr Paul said. 'You can't just ask people for money like that.'

While he'd been listening, Jackson had thought of a good idea. At first, he felt too shy to say anything, but he knew that it was something that Mr Paul would like. And Jackson decided that he really liked Mr Paul. So he took a deep breath and put his hand up.

'Yes, Jackson?' Mr Paul said.

'Um, well, at my old school we had a fundraiser to raise money for a new gym,' Jackson said. 'Maybe we could do that to buy a water tank?'

'What an excellent idea! What kind of fundraising did you do?'

'We had an art show,' Jackson said. 'Everyone did a painting and we had an auction and raised heaps of money.'

'That's fantastic,' Mr Paul said, stroking his chin in a thinking, pleased sort of way. 'We can raise money for a tank to water the oval and the school gardens. I can see that we'll like having you in our class, Jackson. I'm sure the other teachers will want their classes to be a part of such a great idea, too.'

Jackson felt his cheeks heat up again, but this time he didn't look down. Instead he looked right around the classroom.

Lots of kids were smiling at him. He realised his tummy ache had completely gone.

He couldn't wait to tell Sienna at recess!

Chapter Three

When the bell rang for recess, all the kids scraped their chairs back and ran towards the door.

'Don't forget your hats!' Mr Paul called.

'Hey, do you want to play basketball with me and Ned and Bruno?' Luke asked, slapping Jackson on the back.

Sounds like fun! Jackson thought. But then he remembered Sienna.

'Um, nah,' Jackson said. 'Not today, but thanks anyway. I'd better go and find my sister.'

'OK,' said Luke. 'We'll be over by the courts if you're looking for us.'

'Thanks!' said Jackson, and ran off to Sienna's classroom. By the time he got there, he was out of breath.

Sienna was standing with two girls who giggled when they saw him. Jackson always found giggling girls annoying. Sienna wasn't like that at all.

'Hey,' he said to Sienna. 'You'll never guess what my class is doing!'

'Hey, Jack!' Sienna grinned at him. 'Steph, Chloe, this is my brother Jackson.'

'Hi,' said the girls together, and then they giggled again.

Jackson felt his cheeks heat up. He was about to tell Sienna about his idea for the fundraiser, but then Sienna swung her arm over his shoulder and messed up his hair, just like she always did.

She turned to speak to the girls again.

'Hey, is it OK if Jackson hangs out with us?'

Jackson thought this was a silly question. *Why would I need permission?* he wondered. *Girls have so many strange rules and secrets.*

He opened his mouth to talk to Sienna again, but one of the girls shook her head.

'Um, not really,' said the girl, screwing up her face a little.

'Sorry. No boys allowed in our club,' the other one added.

Jackson felt Sienna's whole body tighten. He could tell she was wondering whether she should go with the girls or hang out with him.

I don't want to hang out with them if they don't want me around, he thought. *But they shouldn't make Sienna decide between me and them.*

So before Sienna could say anything, Jackson said quickly, 'Actually, don't worry. I just came over to say hi anyway.'

Jackson had just remembered that Luke had asked him to play basketball. *It's not like I always have to play with Sienna,* he thought.

Sienna looked surprised. 'Are you sure?' she asked.

'Yeah. I'll see you after school, OK?' he said. And he ran over to the basketball courts to find Luke.

Chapter Four

That afternoon, Jackson met Sienna at the school gate. She looked happy to see him. He realised that other than at recess, they hadn't seen each other all day. And since he'd spent practically the whole day having fun with Luke, Ned and Bruno, he'd barely had time to miss Sienna!

'How's your class?' she asked.

But before he could reply, she kept on talking. 'Are you studying the environment, too? My teacher Ms Diamond said that our year level is going to raise money to buy a water tank for the school. We're going to do an art show like we had at school. Oops, I mean at our *old* school.'

Jackson wanted to tell Sienna that the fundraiser had been his idea, but she rambled on. 'I suggested we paint portraits and Ms Diamond loved the idea. So we're all going to do a portrait of someone who inspires us. Great, hey? The auction is next Monday night, so we'll have to work fast!'

Jackson nodded. 'It was my –'

But then their mum pulled up to the

kerb and Sienna ran over to the car before he could finish his sentence.t

On the way home, Jackson sat in the back and stared out the window while Sienna and their mum chatted away in the front. He gazed out at the streets of his new neighbourhood.

Mum and Sienna never stop talking.

Jackson missed where they used to live. He thought of the old horse in the paddock at the corner of their street that always galloped up to the fence to watch the school bus as it rattled past. Then he smiled to himself, remembering the horse joke he'd told Luke at lunchtime. *Why did the horse eat with his mouth open? Because he had bad stable manners!*

During lunch, he and Luke had thought of more and more silly horse jokes. *Why did the horse cross the road? To get to his neigh-bour's house!* They'd both laughed so hard that Luke nearly choked on his sandwich. Jackson smiled to himself again. It had been a good first day at school.

The car pulled into the driveway. Jackson looked at his mum and Sienna. *I can't believe they're still talking*, he thought. *How can two people talk so much?*

'Hey Jackson,' Sienna said, as they walked to the front door. 'Do you want to play Scrabble?'

Jackson was surprised. *That's weird*, he thought. *Sienna thinks Scrabble is boring.* Normally he would've jumped at the chance, but he had lots to do.

'Thanks,' he told her, 'but I might just go and work in my room. I've got stuff to do for tomorrow.' Mr Paul had nominated him and Luke to design a big sign for the art show. Jackson had promised Luke that he'd bring some sketches to school the next day.

Sienna followed him into the house. They dumped their schoolbags inside the front door and made their way in to the kitchen.

'Will you kids be right to make a snack while I just go out to the studio for a bit?' their mum called.

'Sure!' Sienna called. 'Do you want me to make you a chocolate milkshake, Jack?'

'Nah, that's OK,' Jackson said, pushing a chair towards the pantry to reach up to the top shelf. 'I can do it.'

As he put the tin of powdered chocolate and a glass on the bench, he saw that

Sienna had a strange look on her face. *Should I make her a drink, too?* he wondered.

But before he could say anything, she stormed out of the room.

What did I do? Jackson thought, bewildered.

That night at dinner, their mum and dad wanted to know all about their first day at school. Sienna was unusually quiet, so Jackson told them all about Luke and the fundraiser. But when Jackson looked over at Sienna, she was just playing with her spaghetti and looking really annoyed.

Then, at bedtime, she didn't come and jump on his bed like she usually did. She just went straight to her room and closed her door.

I wish I knew what was wrong with her, Jackson thought as he lay in bed. *Maybe things will be better tomorrow.*

Chapter Five

On the way to school the next morning, Sienna was still in a bad mood. Jackson had no idea what he'd done to make her so cross. He was going to tell her the horse joke that Luke had found so funny, but he changed his mind when she frowned at him.

When their mum dropped them at school, Sienna ran off straightaway.

Jackson shrugged to himself, and then he caught sight of Luke and some other boys on the basketball court.

'Hey, guys!' he called, waving as he ran over to them.

'Hey!' Luke said, slapping Jackson's hand in mid-air.

'Hi,' Ned and Bruno said, bouncing the basketball between them and then running off to shoot hoops.

'This is Matt and Tim,' said Luke, pointing to the other boys. 'I was just telling them how funny you are. You're Jokin' Jack. We'll call you JJ.'

Jackson felt his face heat up with pride. He had a nickname! He grinned at Luke.

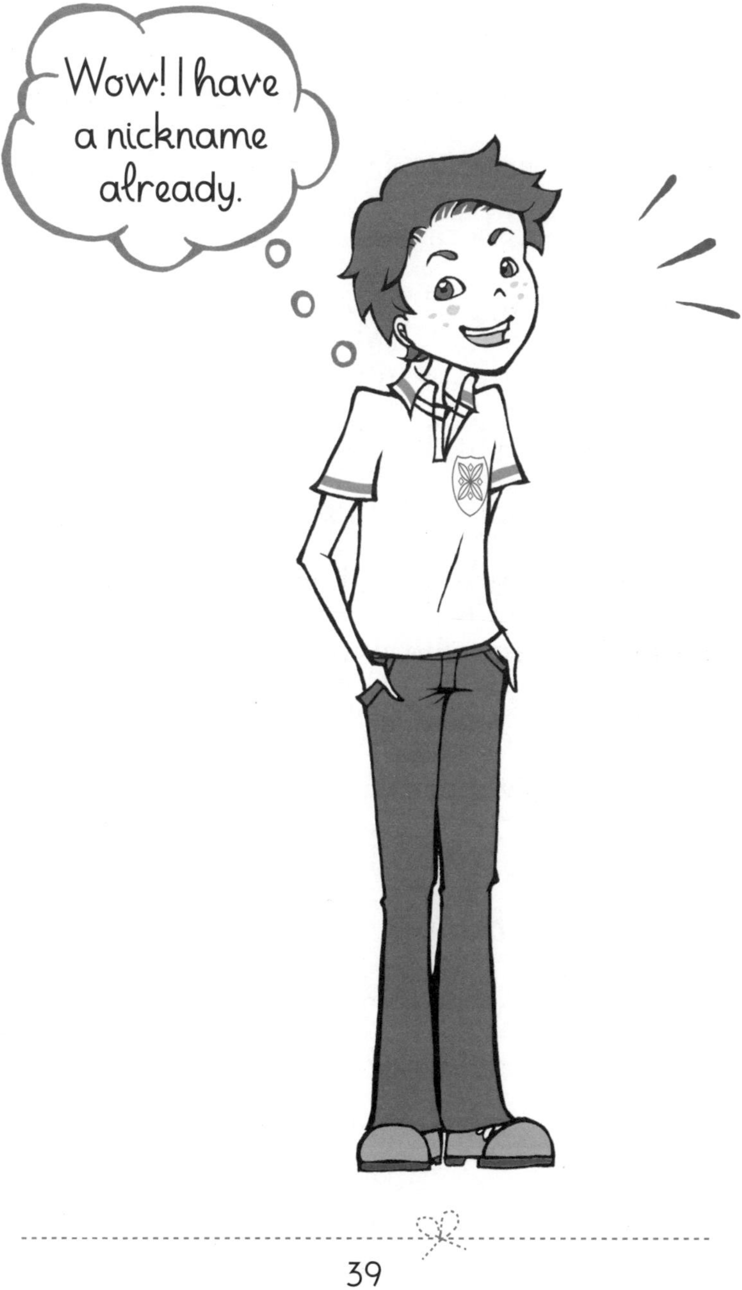
Wow! I have a nickname already.

'That's cool! Hey, I remembered another joke this morning,' Jackson said. 'What do you call a boomerang that won't come back?'

Luke shrugged.

'A stick!' Jackson laughed.

Matt and Tim laughed, too.

'See, I told you!' Luke said to the boys, and he playfully punched Jackson on the shoulder. 'Hey, did you have any ideas for the art show sign?' Luke asked.

'Yeah, I've got my sketchbook here,' Jackson said, pulling it out of his schoolbag. He flicked through the pages to find his sketches.

'Wow, that's cool!' Tim said, pointing to a picture that Jackson had done of a dragon flying over a castle. 'Did you draw all that stuff?'

Jackson nodded, feeling a bit shy all of a sudden. His mum had taught him how to draw dragons.

'You're really good at drawing,' Matt said admiringly. 'I'm only good at drawing cars.'

'I can't draw anything,' Tim said, rolling his eyes. 'Not even a straight line!'

The boys all laughed.

'My mum's a painter,' Jackson explained to the group.

'Cool,' Luke said, impressed.

Jackson was happy that his new friends thought it was cool to have a mum who was an artist. *She might be messy and always running late*, he thought, *but she did teach me how to draw.*

Then the bell rang. The boys walked over to their classroom.

'Hey, JJ,' said Luke, 'do you want to come to my house this afternoon to work on the sign for the art show? We can ask your mum after school.'

'Sure,' said Jackson, feeling excited. He couldn't believe it. It was only his second day at his new school and he'd already been invited to someone's house!

'Hey, Luke,' Jackson whispered, while Mr Paul was writing on the blackboard. 'What do you call a chicken that eats cement?'

Luke shrugged.

'A bricklayer!' Jackson whispered.

Luke snorted.

'Luke,' Mr Paul said, looking over at them, 'do you have the answer for this question?'

'Um, not yet,' Luke said, trying to be serious.

'I'm glad you boys are finding maths so much fun,' Mr Paul said, 'but I'd like you to work more quietly now, please.'

Jackson could hear Luke trying to hold

back his laughter. He knew they should settle down, but there was one more joke he wanted to tell Luke. When Mr Paul had turned to write on the board again, Jackson whispered, 'Why was six afraid of seven?' He paused. 'Because seven ate nine!'

Luke snickered, and Jackson quickly put his head down.

'Right,' Mr Paul said sternly. 'One more sound out of you, Luke, and I'll move you.'

Luke grinned at him, but Jackson felt bad for getting him into trouble. *I'm going to be good from now on*, he decided. *I don't want Luke to be moved away.*

Then Jackson thought about Sienna.

I wonder how she's going in her class without me, he thought.

He had always whispered things to Sienna in class at their old school, but their old teacher had never seemed to mind because they still got their work done. It suddenly felt strange to be in a class without her.

'Anyone got the answer for that second sum yet?' Mr Paul asked, interrupting his thoughts. 'What about you, Jackson?'

Jackson felt himself go red as he quickly looked down at his notebook. He wasn't very good at multiplying. He had worked out the first question, but he didn't know how to do the second.

Just then, Luke whispered the answer to him.

Jackson stared at the sum, and suddenly the numbers made sense. 'Eighty-five!' he said after a second.

'Great!' said Mr Paul. 'Well done.'

Jackson looked over at Luke. He still had his head down, but Jackson could see he was grinning.

'Actually, Mr Paul, Luke helped me with that one,' Jackson said shyly.

'Did he now?' Mr Paul said, staring at them both.

Oops, Jackson thought. *I've done it again! Luke's in trouble.*

'Well, it looks like you work well together, doesn't it?' Mr Paul said. 'You boys can stay sitting together, provided you work quietly, OK?'

'Thanks, Mr Paul!' Jackson said, grinning at Luke.

Chapter Six

That afternoon, when maths had finished, Jackson and Luke ran to the school gate. Sienna ran over a minute later, looking puffed.

'Hi, Sienna!' Jackson said. 'This is my friend, Luke.'

'Hi,' said Sienna, smiling at them both.

Jackson was glad Sienna was happy again. 'I'm going to Luke's house so we

can work on a big sign for the art show,' he told her.

Sienna's smile suddenly disappeared. 'But Mum's taking us shopping, remember?' she frowned.

'To buy *you* a new pencil case,' Jackson reminded her. 'I don't need to come!'

Sienna folded her arms tightly. 'Well, she probably won't let you.'

'I'll ask anyway,' Jackson said with a shrug.

Just then their mum pulled up. Sienna rushed over to the car window.

'Mum,' Sienna said, in a voice that Jackson knew meant she was annoyed, 'Jack wants to go to Luke's house, but we were going to go shopping, weren't we?'

Their mum leant over the front seat and smiled at Jackson and Luke. 'That's a great idea, Jackson. You don't have to come shopping if you don't want to. I'll drop you boys off and make sure it's OK with Luke's mum.'

As they got in the car, Jackson tried to catch Sienna's eye. But she was glaring at Luke, who was picking a scab on his elbow.

When they got to Luke's house, Sienna waited in the car while their mum went inside to talk to Luke's mum. Jackson and Luke ran inside and dumped their schoolbags, said hello to Luke's mum, and then went out into the yard to set up a cricket match.

'Bye, Mum,' Jackson said, as his mum came out of the house. He gave her a wave, hoping she wouldn't come over and kiss him! He didn't want her smooching all over him in front of Luke.

'Bye, love,' his mum called. 'I'll pick you up before dinner.'

'Your mum's nice,' Luke said. 'I don't think your sister likes me much, though.'

'Sienna's OK,' Jackson said. 'She's not like other girls, all giggly and only interested in clothes and stuff. She's actually really cool. Once, at our old house, she built a cubbyhouse just out of bits of wood and sticks and things we found in the backyard. It stayed up for three days until a storm blew it over.'

'Cool,' Luke grinned.

'Another time she caught a frog down at the creek at the back of our place, but Mum felt sorry for it and made us put it back,' Jackson added.

'Wow!' Luke exclaimed. 'You had a creek?'

'Yeah,' Jackson said. 'Our backyard was huge and full of trees. Sometimes kangaroos would come into it from the bush.'

'That's awesome,' Luke said. 'We don't have kangaroos, but we do have a dog.'

Just then a great big chocolate-coloured dog bounded over to Luke, jumping up and licking his face.

'Hey Milo! Milo, *get down!* Milo, this is my friend, JJ,' Luke said, holding one of the dog's paws out for Jackson to shake.

Jackson shook Milo's paw. Milo barked and licked Jackson's face.

'Hey, I'm not an ice-cream!' Jackson laughed.

'He likes you,' Luke said. 'I knew he would.'

'Your dog has good taste,' Jackson grinned.

'Maybe you *do* taste like ice-cream,' Luke joked. 'Vanilla flavour?'

'With sprinkles!' Jackson snorted, pointing to all his freckles.

Chapter Seven

The afternoon passed very quickly. Jackson and Luke played cricket with Milo. Luke's backyard was pretty small, and Luke said that he and his brother had already hit at least ten balls over the fence that month. Milo made a great fielder, except the ball got very slobbery.

When it was almost time for Jackson to get picked up, Luke's mum gave them lemonade and sat outside with them in the shade. Jackson was sweating so much that his eyes stung. He'd left his hat at school and had to borrow a big floppy one from Luke's dad.

He noticed that his arms were already bright pink. He knew he was going to

get in trouble from his mum for getting sunburnt.

'So, are you settling in OK?' Luke's mum asked Jackson. 'Luke tells me you've only been in your new place a few days?'

Jackson nodded.

'Well, it's perfect timing,' Luke's mum said. 'Luke's best friend moved away last year. It's nice that you boys have become friends. You seem like a good influence on Luke.'

Jackson blushed. *She wouldn't think that if she knew how many times I've already got Luke into trouble!* Then Jackson remembered what they were supposed to be doing, instead of playing cricket.

'The art show sign!' he groaned. 'We haven't even started on it and my mum'll be here soon!'

'Oh no,' Luke said, slapping his forehead. 'I can't believe we forgot!'

'How about a sleep-over this weekend?' Luke's mum suggested. 'Then you'll have heaps of time to work on it together.'

'Yeah,' Luke said. 'And we can go down to the soccer oval and kick the ball around!'

'And what about the art show sign?' his mum reminded him.

'*After* we've done the sign,' Luke said with a grin.

'Cool!' said Jackson. But inside he

felt a little nervous at the idea. He had never been to a sleep-over without Sienna before. They'd always done everything together when they lived in the country. 'I'll ask Mum when she gets here.'

'I think that's her now,' Luke's mum said, and she walked through the house to open the front door. 'Luke, show Jackson where the bathroom is so he can wash Milo's slobber off his hands and face! I'll ask your mum about the weekend, Jackson.'

Jackson went and washed his face in the bathroom. His cheeks were pink with heat, but luckily they weren't burnt. He had enough freckles already!

As he stared into the mirror in Luke's

bathroom, Jackson suddenly had an idea about who he was going to paint for his art show portrait.

I have a great idea!

He ran happily down the corridor to see his mum. He had so many things to tell Sienna. He hoped she wasn't *still* in a bad mood with him.

Chapter Eight

For the rest of that week, Jackson and Luke sat next to each other in class every day. Luke was good at maths and Jackson was good at English, so they helped each other a lot. They still told each other jokes, and Mr Paul didn't mind so long as they did their work. In fact, sometimes he wanted to hear their jokes!

'Let's hear a joke, Jackson,' Mr Paul said one afternoon with a grin.

'Why did the toad cross the road?' said Jackson.

Mr Paul shrugged, 'I don't know, Jackson. To get to the other side?'

'Nope,' said Jackson. 'To show his girlfriend he had guts!'

Everybody in the class laughed, including Mr Paul.

Sometimes Mr Paul let them work on their art show portraits during class. Luke sketched his favourite soccer player. Jackson watched the other students draw and paint all kinds of portraits, from their parents to their pets, but he was careful never to draw the face on *his* portrait. He didn't want anyone to know who he was drawing.

'I bet you're painting me,' Luke always joked. 'I'm the person who inspires you the most, aren't I? Cool, good-looking and very talented at basketball and cricket. It's me, isn't it? Hey? Hey?'

Luke even tried to trick Jackson into telling him who he was painting, but Jackson didn't give away any clues.

He would just smile secretly and say, 'You'll see on Monday night!'

That weekend, Jackson's mum drove him over to Luke's house. Jackson started to feel nervous. *What if I have to eat food I don't like? Or what if I have a nightmare? Or I can't find the toilet in the night?*

He was sure Sienna never worried

about stuff like that when she went to sleep-overs.

'Maybe I should just go over for the afternoon, Mum,' Jackson suggested as they got out of the car. 'You could pick me up before dinner.'

'Don't worry, honey, you'll have a great time,' his mum said. 'But if you feel anxious about anything, you just have to call and I can come pick you up. OK?'

'OK,' said Jackson uncertainly.

They rang the bell at the gate and Jackson heard Milo barking loudly. Luke appeared at the gate, holding Milo by his collar. As soon as Jackson saw Luke's goofy grin, he started to feel better.

'Hey, Milo, if you eat me all up now, there will be nothing left for dinner!' Jackson laughed, as the dog jumped up and licked his face.

'You can be his treat,' Luke said. 'After he's eaten all his Meaty Bites!'

'Bye, Mum!' Jackson called, as he ran around the back with Luke and Milo.

'Cricket?' Luke suggested.

'Let's do the art show sign first,' Jackson said. 'I've got some ideas in my sketchbook.' *And I brought my art portrait, too*, he thought, smiling. *Just in case Sienna decides to go snooping in my room!* He didn't want Luke to see it either, so he left it in his bag.

The boys worked hard on the sign all afternoon. It was lots of fun. By the time they finished, it was almost dark outside.

'Gee! I knew Luke was a good drawer,' Luke's dad said, when he saw the sign. 'But you're really good, too, Jackson.'

Luke's good at drawing too.

'His mum's a painter,' Luke said, nodding. 'She taught JJ how to draw.'

'Oh, that explains it, then,' Luke's dad said.

Jackson didn't need to worry about not liking Luke's mum's cooking because they ordered takeaway Hawaiian pizza – his favourite. Then they stayed up late to watch a funny DVD.

Jackson was excited to see two sleeping bags on the floor in Luke's room. They could pretend they were camping! And even though it took Jackson ages to fall asleep, he didn't mind. Luke's breathing in the dark reminded him of sharing a bedroom with Sienna at their old house.

When Jackson did fall asleep, though, he had the strangest dream. He dreamt that when he looked in the mirror he saw Sienna's face instead of his.

Chapter
Nine

The next morning, Jackson and Luke had yummy bacon and eggs for breakfast. Luke poured maple syrup on his bacon, and Jackson copied him. It was delicious!

Then Luke's dad took them to the soccer oval. Luke's brother, Harry, and his dog, Milo, came along, and they all played soccer until lunchtime.

Luke's mum drove Jackson home on Sunday afternoon. Jackson was excited about seeing Sienna and telling her all about his weekend. *But I'll have to sneak my portrait into my room so she doesn't see it*, he reminded himself. *It's still top-secret!*

When Jackson got to the front door, Sienna was there waiting for him. 'Hey, so what did you do at Luke's?' she asked, following him down the hall.

'Um, not much,' said Jackson, not looking at Sienna. He wanted to tell her about his weekend, but he had to hide his portrait somewhere safe first.

But Sienna sped up and stood at the foot of the stairs, blocking his way.

'You must have done something!' she insisted. 'What did you play?'

'Can you move, please?' Jackson said. 'I have to go to my room.' He pushed past Sienna to walk up the stairs.

'I'm talking to you!' Sienna shouted loudly. 'It's very rude to just ignore me.'

'Oi, you two!' their dad called from the lounge room. 'No shouting.'

Jackson suddenly felt very angry. He went upstairs to his room and closed the door. He had a feeling that Sienna had been in his room, and he looked around carefully. *She HAS been in here*, he thought, shaking his head. *I left that drawer open yesterday, and now it's closed. Lucky I took my portrait with me.*

He pulled out his rolled-up portrait and was just about to hide it when Sienna started banging on the door.

'You can't come in,' Jackson called, shoving the portrait under his bed.

'Yes, I can!' Sienna growled, throwing open the door.

'That is *not* fair!' Jackson yelled, standing up quickly. 'We're not allowed into each other's rooms without permission. It was *you* who made up that rule and now *you're* the one who's breaking it! This is my room!'

Sienna took a step forward, looking at him suspiciously. 'You're hiding something!' she said. 'You and Luke have done something bad, haven't you?'

'It's none of your business!' Jackson shouted. 'And why would we do something bad? You don't even *know* Luke. You don't want to talk to me anymore, and now that

I've finally got my own friend, you're mean about him!'

'Kids, what is all that yelling about?' their dad called.

'Sorry, Dad,' Sienna called back. Then she said more quietly, 'What do you mean I don't want to talk to you anymore? You're the one who's always running away from me, and hiding in your room, and going to Luke's house!'

'You didn't want to hang out with me, remember?' Jackson said, still feeling angry. 'You wanted me to make my own friends. Plus *your* friends said "no boys allowed". And besides, I've been trying to talk to you all week but you never listen.'

When he saw Sienna's face, he felt bad for shouting at her. She looked very sad all of a sudden.

'I'm sorry,' said Sienna in a low voice. 'You're right. I thought you didn't want to hang out with me now that you have Luke. And I've missed you – it was so boring this weekend without you here.'

Jackson couldn't believe his ears. 'Really? I missed you, too. I was worried I'd have a bad dream and you wouldn't be there to make me feel better.'

'Sorry, little bro,' Sienna said. She smiled at her twin and ruffled his hair. 'Maybe you should have told Luke to invite me, too.'

Jackson poked out his tongue.

'Hey, why don't we sleep in the same room tonight, like we used to?' Sienna said. 'You can put your mattress on my floor. In fact,' she added excitedly, 'it's been ages since we had a midnight feast.'

Jackson shook his head. 'Oh, I'm not sure,' he said in a serious voice, and Sienna's face fell. Then he grinned. 'There's no way we'll fit a mattress in your room – there's too much mess! Let's do it in my room instead.'

Chapter Ten

On Monday evening, the night of the art show, Jackson dressed in his lucky yellow T-shirt. He felt nervous about the art exhibition, but happy that he and Sienna had made up. He hoped she'd like his portrait.

I wonder who she painted? he thought as he got ready. *I've been so busy hiding mine that I forgot to look for hers!*

Sienna came into his room without knocking, but this time he didn't mind. She just sat on his bed and watched him wrestle with his sticky-up hair.

I wish my hair would sit flat.

Out of the corner of his eye, Jackson saw her fiddling with her bracelet. Jackson knew she only fiddled with it when she was a little bit nervous. *She wants to tell me something*, Jackson thought. *Maybe she thinks my hair looks stupid?*

'You're wearing that T-shirt?' Sienna asked, raising an eyebrow.

'Yeah, I thought I'd wear my lucky T-shirt because it's a special night,' Jackson said, still trying to smooth down some of the most sticky-up bits of his hair with spit. 'It would be great if the exhibition earned enough money to buy the water tank, wouldn't it?'

Sienna sighed. 'You know what, Jack? Yellow's not such a great colour on redheads.'

'Really?' Jackson said, looking back in the mirror. It looked OK to him.

'It's just that, you know, with our red hair and pale skin,' Sienna said slowly, 'well, all those bright colours together are fine for painting, but not really for wearing.'

'Oh,' said Jackson.

I like these colours, he thought, *but I guess she knows more about fashion.* He shrugged and started taking his T-shirt off. *I'll just wear my blue T-shirt, then.*

He didn't really care that much, but he didn't want to embarrass Sienna. Especially now that they were friends again!

Then suddenly, Sienna sat up straight and said, 'Actually, Jack, you should wear it. We just have different taste, that's all!'

'Really?' Jackson said, looking at himself in the mirror again. Now he was really confused! 'Well, it *is* my lucky T-shirt …'

'You know what?' she laughed. 'You're so daggy that you're cool!'

Jackson didn't know if that was good or bad, but he just shook his head and pulled his yellow top back on. Girls were just too difficult to try to work out.

Why does she worry so much about being cool, anyway? he wondered. *It's like she wants to be the same as everyone else — but as different to me as possible!*

'I don't care if I'm cool or not, really,' he told Sienna. 'I'd rather my friends think

I'm funny than cool. To be funny, you just have to be yourself.'

Sienna got a strange look on her face. Then she jumped off the bed and gave Jackson a huge hug. 'You're the best!' she said, ruffling his hair.

'Hey!' he said. 'You're messing it up!'

'Wear it messy!' Sienna said over her shoulder, striding out of Jackson's bedroom. 'It makes you look like *you*!'

Jackson looked in the mirror. Now that Sienna had messed his hair up again, he was probably never going to get it to lie flat. He made a silly face in the mirror, and then he ran downstairs to make sure their mum wasn't running late!

Jackson, Sienna and their mum and dad pulled into the school car park. They were running late as usual and the car park was almost full.

'Looks like a good turnout,' their dad said, as he drove slowly around the grounds, looking for a park. 'Might get that water tank, kids!'

'You two are suspiciously quiet,' their mum said, twisting around in the front seat to look at them. 'You're not fighting, are you?'

Sienna grabbed Jackson's hand and squeezed it.

He smiled at her. Jackson knew Sienna was just as excited as he was. He could tell how she was feeling. That was the great thing about being twins. He'd thought that maybe because they were growing up that they were growing apart, but now he was sure they were closer than ever.

'OK, here we are,' their dad said, pulling into a tight park. 'You know, I haven't even seen your portraits. Have you?' he asked their mum.

'Nobody has,' their mum replied. 'It's a secret. I asked the kids who they'd painted, but they wouldn't tell me. They haven't even told each other!'

'Really?' their dad chuckled. 'That's a first. Usually these two know everything about each other.'

Well, maybe not everything, Jackson thought. *We are twins, but we are still different.*

Sienna looked at Jackson and smiled.

He knew she was thinking the same thing.

Inside, Jackson found Mr Paul and introduced him to his mum and dad. Jackson wanted to get a good seat, but his parents kept chatting to Mr Paul.

Jackson craned his neck, looking around for Luke, but he couldn't see him anywhere. *He's probably already inside getting a good seat!* Jackson thought.

They were nearly inside when Jackson saw Steph and Chloe walking towards them. *Oh no*, Jackson thought. *I really wanted to sit next to Sienna, but now she'll probably want to sit with her new friends.*

Then he heard his mum ask Sienna if she wanted to sit with the girls.

'Nah,' Sienna replied. 'I think I'll sit next to Jack tonight.'

Jackson couldn't believe his ears. He felt so happy he couldn't stop smiling.

I love being a twin.

go girl

flip it!

Flip to
Sienna's
Side...

...if you haven't read it yet!

Once you've read both sides, cut open carefully along the line to read the secret chapter!

Only open after you've read both sides of the story.

Secret Chapter!

flip it!

go out

hardie grant EGMONT

Sienna's Side

flip it!

go girl

Twin Trouble
first published in 2009
this edition published in 2014 by
Hardie Grant Egmont
Ground Floor, Building 1, 658 Church Street
Richmond, Victoria 3121, Australia
www.hardiegrantegmont.com.au

A CiP record for this title is available from the National Library of Australia

Text copyright © 2009 Sally Rippin
Illustration and design copyright © 2014 Hardie Grant Egmont

Illustration by Aki Fukuoka
Design by Michelle Mackintosh
Text design and typesetting by Ektavo

Printed in China by WKT

1 3 5 7 9 10 8 6 4 2

go girl

flip it!

Twin Trouble

by
Sally Rippin

Illustrations by
Aki Fukuoka

hardie grant EGMONT

Chapter One

'OK!' Sienna's mum called. 'Time to go!'

Sienna came hurtling down the front stairs of their new house. Today was the first day at her new school. *I can't wait to meet the kids in my class!* she thought. She tingled with excitement as she ran down the steps towards the car, beating her twin brother, Jackson, by seconds.

'I win *again*! You've got to speed up, little bro,' she teased.

Even though they were twins, Sienna was four minutes older and was five

centimetres taller than Jackson. As far as she was concerned, that made her the big sister. It was a good enough reason to tease her *little* brother whenever she could.

'Looks like I get the front seat again,' she said, grinning.

'Come on, kids,' their mum said. 'You can both hop in the back.'

'But all your canvasses are still in there,' Jackson complained.

'Oh, I forgot,' their mum said. 'Well, we haven't got time to get them out now. You can get in the front, Sienna. Jackson, just push that stuff onto the floor, love.'

Sienna giggled. She liked that their car was such a mess. There were always

paintbrushes and sticks and shells and other treasures that their mum had collected, all rattling around on the floor. Sienna loved that their mum was an artist and that she looked different to other mums, with her swishy skirts and long hair.

In fact, Sienna always wished that she'd inherited their mum's dark hair and olive skin. Instead, she and her brother had their dad's ginger hair, pale skin and freckles.

At least my hair is straight, Sienna thought, *not sticking up everywhere like Jack's.*

She turned around in her seat to look at Jackson, with his sticky-up hair and sticky-out ears. *We're so different*, Sienna thought.

Jackson was really good at English, but Sienna liked maths and science. Jackson was quiet and shy. He never wanted to do anything without Sienna, but Sienna loved meeting new people. They had their own rooms at their new house, but when they had shared a room at their old house, all of Jackson's books and toys were always put away neatly. Sienna's stuff was always everywhere!

I'm glad we're going to be in different classes, Sienna thought. Their old school had been so small that they'd had to be in the same class. They'd always sat together and had all the same friends. She hoped Jackson wouldn't be too shy to make his

I want to make new friends.

own friends at their new school. *I just want to be known as Sienna*, she thought. *I'm sick of always being known as just one of the twins.*

Chapter Two

When they got to school, Sienna and her mum found Sienna's classroom and met her new teacher, Ms Diamond. Sienna liked Ms Diamond straightaway. *She's so nice*, Sienna thought to herself.

Jackson waited in the corridor for their mum. Then he and their mum went off to find his class.

Sienna stood at the front of the class while Ms Diamond got everyone's attention.

'Welcome back, kids,' Ms Diamond said warmly. 'I hope you all had a great holiday.'

Sienna looked around the classroom as everyone talked excitedly. She saw lots of girls she liked the look of. *I wonder who's funny, and who's friendly, and who's the kind of girl you can talk to on the phone for hours?* She smiled at a girl who looked really nice – she had long hair up in a ponytail and a very friendly face. The girl grinned back.

'Shoosh, everyone,' said Ms Diamond. 'There's plenty of time to talk later. I'd like to introduce you to our new student, Sienna Hartford. I know you'll all make her feel welcome.'

Sienna felt her cheeks grow warm, and little butterflies of excitement flitted around in her stomach.

'Can I have two volunteers to look after Sienna until she's settled in?' Ms Diamond asked.

Lots of kids put their hands up, but Ms Diamond picked the girl Sienna had smiled at, and her friend next to her. 'Ah, Chloe and Steph. Thank you, girls.'

Sienna's heart soared, and she smiled gratefully at Ms Diamond. It was exciting making new friends.

But even so, she found herself thinking of Jackson. She hoped he had lots of kids to look after him, too.

Ms Diamond pushed Sienna gently in the direction of the girls. 'Matt, do you mind moving up a seat, so that Sienna can

sit next to Chloe? Thank you. OK, now, let's have a look at what we're going to study this term.'

Sienna wound her way through the desks to the place where Chloe and Steph were clearing a space for her. They smiled as she sat down.

'Hi!' said the girl with the ponytail. 'I'm Chloe. And this is Steph. We love your hair!'

Sienna touched her hair, amazed.

Steph must have seen her expression, because she added, 'Yeah, strawberry blonde is a beautiful colour.'

'Strawberry blonde hair and freckles are so in!' Chloe giggled.

Sienna couldn't help feeling surprised. *Red hair and freckles?* she wondered. *Are they joking?* She looked at the girls uncertainly, but they just smiled back at her. It looked like they were being serious.

Sienna had never liked her red hair much. It was so different to all of her friends' hair. But nobody had ever called it strawberry blonde before. That made it sound much more interesting!

She felt like her face might split from smiling. 'Thanks,' she said, feeling unusually embarrassed. 'I like yours, too. Both of you.'

'OK, girls,' Ms Diamond said kindly, from the front of the class. 'You'll have

lots of time during recess to get to know each other. Now, who can tell me what our project is for this term? Remember, we talked about it during the last assembly of the year?'

There was a pause, then some murmuring, and finally a boy put his hand up. 'Yes, Joey?' said Ms Diamond.

'The planets?'

'No, that was last term, Joey, good try. Anyone else remember?' She looked around. 'No? Well, here it is.'

Sienna watched Ms Diamond write in large letters on the board.

The Environment

At Sienna's old school they had talked a lot about the environment. She would have loads of ideas!

'Can anyone tell me what some of our environmental concerns are?' Ms Diamond asked, looking around the classroom.

Sienna quickly put her hand up. She wanted to make a good impression on her first day.

'Yes, Sienna?' Ms Diamond asked.

'Climate change?' Sienna offered.

'Excellent! That's exactly what we're going to be talking about this term – what climate change is, and how it affects us. Thank you, Sienna.'

'I'm so glad you're sitting next to us,' Chloe whispered.

Sienna glowed with happiness. She hoped that Jackson's class was studying the same topic, too. She would have to remember to ask him at recess.

'OK, listen carefully,' Ms Diamond said.

'I want you to get into groups of three or four, and write down things we can do to save our environment. Obviously, it's good to include some big ideas, but also think of some smaller things we can do ourselves.'

Sienna put her hand up again. 'Like turning off lights when you leave the room?' she suggested.

'That's exactly the sort of thing I mean,' said Ms Diamond. Now, write a list in your groups and we'll compare them at the end of the lesson.'

Sienna pulled a new exercise book out of her bag and a sharp pencil from her old tartan pencil case. When she looked up, both Steph and Chloe were staring

at her. Then they looked at each other.

'Should we ask her?' Chloe asked.

'Yeah, definitely,' Steph said.

'Ask me what?' Sienna asked, suddenly feeling nervous.

'Well, we wondered if you want to be in our club?' Steph asked.

'Yeah, you seem really nice,' added Chloe.

'Um, OK, thanks!' Sienna said, smiling at them.

Then she noticed that Chloe and Steph had matching pink, sparkly pencil cases. She'd wanted a new pencil case, but things had been so crazy since her family had moved house that she hadn't had a chance to ask her mum yet.

I wonder if I'll be allowed to get a new one, she thought. *It would be cool to have the same one as my new friends. Then I'll REALLY feel part of their club!*

'We liked you as soon as we saw you,' Steph continued.

'And you have a cool name,' added Chloe.

Maybe I won't tell them that Mum named me after a tube of brown paint, then, Sienna thought to herself, trying not to giggle.

'OK, girls, it's time to work now,' said Ms Diamond, coming up behind them.

Sienna jumped. She felt bad that they hadn't written anything down yet. She didn't want Ms Diamond to think that she

was naughty. She looked over at Steph and Chloe, but they still hadn't even opened their books.

'Shall I start writing some stuff down?' Sienna suggested.

'Sure,' said Steph. 'How about turning out the lights?'

'That was Sienna's idea!' Chloe said, nudging her with her elbow.

'It's all right,' said Sienna, remembering all the things that she'd learnt at her old school about saving the environment. 'There's heaps we can add. Like turning down the heating.'

'And riding a bike to school,' Steph suggested.

'How about fixing a leaky tap? We've got one at home,' said Chloe.

'This is cool! We've got so many good ideas,' said Sienna, writing them down.

Sienna's first day of school was turning out just how she'd wanted it to. She was having fun and making friends. She couldn't wait to tell Jackson at recess!

Chapter Three

The bell rang for recess and Sienna put down her pencil.

'All right,' Ms Diamond said. 'We'll come back to this after the break. Don't forget your hats!'

'Come on,' Steph said. 'We'll show you around.'

'Yeah,' Chloe said, 'you'll need to know

which boys are OK and which ones to avoid!'

'Thanks,' Sienna said as the girls walked out of the classroom. 'And I'll introduce you to my ... brother!'

She'd been about to say 'twin', but then she remembered that she didn't want to be known as 'one of the twins' anymore.

Just then, Jackson came running up to Sienna, a huge grin on his face.

Sienna couldn't help herself – seeing his goofy grin made her laugh.

'Hey, you'll never guess what my class is doing!' Jackson panted. He was out of breath from running across the courtyard.

'Hey, Jack!' Sienna grinned at him.

'Steph, Chloe, this is my brother Jackson.'

'Hi,' the girls said together, and then they giggled.

Sienna didn't really want Jackson hanging around, but she felt a bit sorry for him, being on his own on their first day.

'Hey, is it OK if Jackson hangs out with us?' she said to Chloe and Steph, swinging one arm over Jackson's shoulder and messing up his hair with her free hand.

Jackson automatically flattened his hair with both hands, like he always did.

Steph looked at Chloe. Chloe looked back at Steph. It felt like a long time passed, then Sienna saw Steph shake her head slightly.

Sienna felt her cheeks begin to heat up even before they answered.

Steph spoke first. 'Um, not really,' she said, screwing her face up a little.

'Sorry. No boys allowed in our club,' Chloe added.

Sienna's stomach sank. She felt Jackson's shoulders slump under her arm. Sienna looked back at Chloe and Steph.

Chloe was twirling her ponytail awkwardly. Steph was avoiding her eyes, looking out over the playground.

Sienna knew she had to choose between her new friends and her brother. Suddenly she felt annoyed with Jackson. *Why should I feel bad?* she thought. *This is my chance to make new friends. Jack should go and make his own friends.*

She was about to turn around to tell him this when Jackson said quickly, 'Actually, don't worry. I just came over to say hi anyway.'

Sienna stared at Jackson, amazed, but he'd already slipped out from under her arm.

'Are you sure?' she asked.

'Yeah. I'll see you after school, OK?' Without looking back, Jackson jogged off over the asphalt.

Sienna watched him go. *He doesn't even seem upset*, she thought.

'Let's go and sit over in our spot. It's so hot already!' said Steph.

'Yeah,' Chloe agreed. 'It must be a hundred degrees! Hey, look, there's Ned playing basketball.'

The two girls giggled.

'Chloe likes him!' Steph told Sienna.

'I do *not!*' Chloe frowned. 'I just think he's good at basketball, that's all.'

Sienna followed the girls over to a bench under a tree. It was good to get out of the sun. She really didn't want any more freckles. But as they sat down, she kept looking over at Jackson. He was laughing with some boys on the basketball courts.

Part of her felt strange without him. At their old school, they'd always played together. *But now it's time for us to make our own friends*, she reminded herself.

Then she remembered that she hadn't even listened to what he wanted to tell her! She felt bad, so she decided to make it up to him after school. She'd make him

a special milkshake with extra chocolate, just how he liked it. *And we can even play a game of boring old Scrabble*, she thought, *because Jackson likes it*.

Chapter Four

That afternoon, Sienna met Jackson at the school gate where their mum was going to pick them up.

'How's your class?' Sienna asked, still feeling bad about what had happened at recess. 'Are you studying the environment, too? My teacher Ms Diamond said that our year level is going to raise money to buy

a water tank for the school. We're going to do an art show like we had at school. Oops, I mean at our *old* school. I suggested we paint portraits and Ms Diamond loved the idea. So we're all going to do a portrait of someone who inspires us. Great, hey? The auction is next Monday night, so we'll have to work fast!'

Jackson nodded. 'It was my —'

But then Sienna saw their mum's car pull in to the kerb. She pulled Jackson by the hand. 'Quick! There's Mum!' she said.

'Hello, darlings!' their mum called. 'One of you hop in the front. I still haven't taken those canvasses out of the back yet.'

Sienna climbed into the front seat next

to their mum. She chatted excitedly about all the things that had happened on her first day. It was only as they pulled into their street that she remembered to tell their mum about the art show.

'How fabulous!' their mum exclaimed. 'Just like at your old school! You can both use my studio to work in, if you like. I've got some lovely new watercolour paints you might like to try.'

'We have to do a portrait,' Sienna explained. 'We have to choose someone who inspires us.'

'Oh, that's a great theme,' their mum said. 'What a good idea. You could paint your favourite artist, Sienna – Frida Kahlo.

Remember I painted her on that T-shirt for you? Who are you going to do, Jackson, love?'

But Jackson hadn't heard. He was staring out the car window, daydreaming. Sienna and their mum looked at each other and smiled. Then Sienna turned to look at Jackson again, and realised that maybe he didn't look so happy after all.

Maybe he's cross at me for not hanging out with him today, she thought.

When they got home, Sienna remembered that she was going to be especially nice to Jackson to make up for deserting him at school. But he didn't want to play Scrabble with her. And when

she offered to make him a milkshake, he turned her down!

That's a bit rude, she thought, staring at Jackson as he climbed onto a chair to reach the powdered chocolate. He took the tin down from the top shelf of the pantry and put it on the bench.

He's definitely mad at me for not hanging out with him at school, Sienna thought, frowning. *Well, if that's the way he wants to be, he can make his own milkshake!* She felt so cross that she turned around and stomped out of the kitchen and up to her bedroom.

At dinner that evening, Sienna still felt grumpy. She told their mum and dad all

about Ms Diamond and Chloe and Steph. She asked their mum about getting a new pencil case, too, and their mum said they could go shopping the next day.

She wanted to tell their parents about her ideas for the environment, too, but it seemed that they only wanted to hear Jackson's news. She knew that they were worried he'd be too shy to make friends. But when Jackson told them about his new friend Luke, that was all they wanted to talk about! And Jackson talked about the art show fundraiser like it was all *his* idea.

Sienna felt frustrated. As soon as she'd finished her spaghetti, she ran straight up to her bedroom and shut the door.

Why won't Mum and Dad listen to me?

I know I should be happy that Jack had a good first day, Sienna thought as she lay on her bed, *but it was my first day of school, too!*

Chapter Five

The next day, Sienna still felt cross with Jackson. On the car ride to school, Sienna sat in the front without asking – even though their mum had remembered to clear out the back seat so that they could both sit there. Sienna felt way too annoyed with Jackson to sit next to him. And when they reached the school gate, Sienna ran ahead without even saying goodbye.

She could see Chloe and Steph under the tree on their special bench. She ran over to them.

As she got closer, she saw that they were both wearing braids in their hair.

How did they know to wear their hair like that? Did they talk last night? Sienna thought, her heart sinking. *Am I still part of their club?* She ran up to the bench, her tummy in knots.

'Hey, Sienna!' Chloe said, looking pleased to see her. 'Steph and I have just been doing each other's hair. Do you want us to do yours?'

Sienna breathed a sigh of relief and smiled at the girls. *They haven't left me out*

on purpose, she realised. *I'm just being silly!*

'That would be cool,' she said. 'Thanks!'

'Oh no, I don't think we have time,' Steph frowned. 'Bell's about to go.'

'Doesn't matter, just come early tomorrow!' Chloe said. 'We'll all do each other's.'

'Yeah, so we can all look the same!' said Steph.

'OK,' Sienna said, as the bell rang.

On the way to their classroom, Sienna noticed that the girls had matching pink, sparkly ribbons in their hair.

It would be so nice to have the same ribbons as them, Sienna thought. *Then we'd be like a real club, even though I'm only new.*

How was she going to convince her mum to take her to school earlier the next morning *and* buy her some hair ribbons as well as a new pencil case?

Then Sienna thought, *I'm being silly! I've never cared about this kind of thing before.*

At her old school, Sienna had never worried about what she looked like, and she had always fitted in there.

I don't know why it's different here, she thought. *Is it because I'm not in the same class as Jackson?*

Sienna loved Ms Diamond. She was pretty and fun, but she still made them work hard. This was good because Steph and Chloe seemed to chat a lot. Mainly about clothes and boys, or anything except the

subject Ms Diamond was trying to teach!

'Steph, Chloe, heads down now, please,' Ms Diamond would gently remind them when they were supposed to be working.

I wonder how Jack's going, Sienna thought, forgetting that she had been cross with him that morning.

She thought about how they'd always sat next to each other at their old school. It felt strange to be in a class without him. They'd always helped each other with their work. She hoped he'd be able to do his maths without her. She would miss him in English! He always knew how to spell hard words.

Their dad said that they made a great

team. They were good at different things, but they were both good at drawing and at helping each other.

'Very good, Sienna!' said Ms Diamond, interrupting her thoughts. She was wandering around the class to see how everyone was going with the questions.

She leant over Sienna's shoulder, looking at her work. 'These are excellent answers,' she said. 'Well done.'

Sienna blushed. 'Thanks,' she said. 'Some of this we – I mean – I did already at my old school.'

'Keep up the good work,' Ms Diamond said, smiling.

She moved over to Chloe's desk. 'Hmm, Chloe,' Sienna heard Ms Diamond say quietly. 'I think you've multiplied instead of divided here. Maybe try it again.'

Sienna saw Chloe's cheeks redden and she felt sorry for her. 'Chloe, I can help you if you want,' she whispered.

Chloe smiled. 'That would be great!

I'm not very good at maths. I'm so glad you're my friend.'

Sienna grinned back. 'Me, too,' she said.

As they packed up their maths books after class, Ms Diamond reminded them about their portraits.

I'll see if Jack wants to work on them together after school! Sienna thought.

Chapter Six

After school, Sienna waved goodbye to Steph and Chloe. She looked for Jackson in the playground, but she couldn't see him anywhere. Then she saw him standing by the school gate.

Sienna ran over to him. She was about to ask him if he wanted to work on their portraits together when she saw that he was standing with another boy.

'Hi, Sienna!' Jackson said. 'This is my friend, Luke.'

'Hi,' said Sienna, smiling at them. She hadn't realised how much she'd missed Jackson that day.

Luke grinned back at Sienna. He had a nice, cheeky smile.

'I'm going to Luke's house so we can work on a big sign for the art show,' Jackson said, looking pleased.

Sienna frowned. *I can't believe he's going to a friend's house. Chloe and Steph haven't even asked me over yet.*

'But Mum's taking us shopping,' she said, starting to feel annoyed all over again. 'Remember?'

Mum won't let you go.

'To buy *you* a new pencil case,' Jackson reminded her. 'I don't need to come!'

'Well, she probably won't let you,' Sienna said to Jackson, folding her arms.

Jackson just shrugged. 'I'll ask anyway.'

When their mum pulled up, Sienna rushed over to the car. 'Mum,' she said quickly, 'Jack wants to go to Luke's

house, but we were going to go shopping, weren't we?'

Their mum peered out the window at Jackson and Luke. 'That's a great idea, Jackson. You don't have to come shopping if you don't want to. I'll drop you boys off and make sure it's OK with Luke's mum.'

Sienna looked at her mum in surprise. *She doesn't even know Luke and she's letting Jack go to his house?*

As they got in the car, Sienna looked at Luke. He was picking at a scab on his elbow.

Sometimes boys are so gross, she thought.

'What lovely manners Luke has!' Sienna's mum said after they had dropped

the boys off. 'Isn't it great that Jackson's already made such a good friend?'

Sienna frowned and stared out the window. It *was* good that Jackson had Luke, but at the same time she sort of wished things were like they used to be.

Everything's changed.

Chapter Seven

At the shopping centre, Sienna and her mum found a really cool purple pencil case with silver stars on it. With her pocket money, Sienna bought some sparkly pink ribbons just like Steph and Chloe's.

Sienna was feeling much better. She couldn't wait to show the girls what she'd bought.

Sienna and her mum carried their shopping bags down to the food court.

'This is nice, isn't it?' her mum said as they carried their hot chocolates and muffins to a table. 'Just the girls!'

'It sure is!' Sienna agreed, sipping her hot chocolate.

Sienna liked having her mum all to herself, but she really missed Jackson, too. Jackson didn't like shopping, especially in busy shopping centres, but he made it fun by making up silly stories about the other shoppers. It was their little game. If Sienna laughed at his stories, Jackson got a point. If she managed to keep a straight face, Sienna got a point.

I wonder what Jack and Luke are up to, she thought, as she stirred her drink. *And I wonder when Steph or Chloe will ask me over to their houses?*

Just then, Sienna remembered that

Steph and Chloe had suggested they all wear pink T-shirts to the art auction on Monday night.

'Mum,' she said, 'you know that pink sparkly T-shirt we saw? The one I really liked?'

Sienna's mum looked at her over the top of her coffee cup. 'Yes,' she said. 'It was very different to what you usually wear, wasn't it?'

Sienna looked down into the froth at the bottom of her cup. 'Yeah, I guess so,' she mumbled.

'Does this have something to do with Chloe and Steph?' her mum asked, raising an eyebrow.

'Well, sort of,' Sienna said. 'We all want to wear matching T-shirts to the art auction.'

Her mum looked at her thoughtfully, and then she said, 'But I love the outfits you usually wear. They're so unique.'

'Please, Mum? I really want to match Chloe and Steph.'

'Well, I suppose. We could make it an early birthday present for you.'

Sienna smiled. 'Thanks so much, Mum!' she said happily, leaning over to give her a hug.

Chapter Eight

Chloe and Steph loved Sienna's new pencil case. Chloe even said that she wanted one as well!

All that week, Sienna worked hard in class and hung out with Steph and Chloe during recess and lunch.

Chloe and Steph spent a lot of time talking about boys and clothes, which

was OK some of the time, but Sienna also missed hanging out with Jackson.

Steph and Chloe didn't have brothers, so they didn't really know how to act around boys. But Sienna knew that boys were not that different to girls in a lot of ways. She should know – she'd shared her whole life with a boy! And he wasn't that strange.

Sometimes I think I'm more like Jack than Chloe and Steph, she thought as they walked around the playground together.

Jackson and Sienna liked doing lots of the same things, like building cubbyhouses and playing basketball. *But maybe that's just because we're twins*, Sienna wondered.

And anyway, I want to be friends with Steph and
Chloe and do more girly things, too!

Sienna would sometimes watch Jackson

in the courtyard playing basketball with Luke and the other boys. She often felt like joining in. She was actually pretty good at basketball.

But when she suggested joining in to Steph and Chloe, they complained that the boys got so sweaty and smelly that they stank out the whole classroom. And maybe Jackson didn't want her hanging around, anyway.

Before school each day, Sienna, Steph and Chloe would do each other's hair. They tried all different styles. On Wednesday, it was braids. Then on Thursday it was funny side ponytails. Sienna always wore the ribbon, though. She knew it was a

bit silly, but it made her feel more like she belonged.

Sienna didn't see that much of Jackson all week, because after school he usually went to his room to work on his portrait. He was keeping his painting a secret from her, so she wasn't even allowed to talk to him while he worked.

Sienna hadn't started her portrait yet. She couldn't think of anyone to paint. It was supposed to be someone who inspired her, but there wasn't anyone she felt right about painting. *I love Mum and Dad, but I don't want to choose between them.* She wondered if she should do Frida Kahlo, her favourite artist, but that didn't feel quite right, either.

She knew that Chloe was painting her favourite movie star, because she loved acting. Steph was painting an Olympic swimmer. But Sienna couldn't think of any famous people who inspired her. Plus her mum always said that a really good portrait showed what was inside a person, not just what they looked like. Sienna had no idea what was inside any of those people in magazines, really, because she'd never met them!

On Friday morning, while Sienna was doing her hair in the bathroom mirror, she suddenly had the best idea. *I know exactly who to paint*, she grinned to herself. *I've just thought of the perfect person!*

That weekend Jackson went to stay with Luke, and Sienna spent her first full weekend without her twin. Even though Jackson was quiet, the house felt strange and a bit lonely without him.

'Why don't you come into my studio to finish off your portrait, love?' Sienna's mum asked. 'It's due on Monday, isn't it?'

'It's OK, I'm almost finished,' Sienna said. 'And anyway, I don't want you seeing it yet. It's going to be a surprise.'

'Well, I'll be in my studio if you need me, and Dad will be home soon. We can get pizza and a DVD tonight, if you like?'

Sienna knew her mum was trying to cheer her up, but the truth was that Sienna just missed Jackson. There was nothing her mum could say that would make Sienna feel better.

I thought I wanted us to have our own lives, but now it feels like half of me is missing, she

thought miserably. *And Jack is so fun to hang out with.*

Sienna wandered into Jackson's room. She smiled to see how neat it was. As

always, all the Lego models he had built were in a straight line along the top of his bookcase, and all his books were stacked. Nothing was on the floor, and his bed had been made.

We really are opposites, Sienna thought. *My room is so messy that I can never find anything.* Then she realised something. *Jack must love having a room to himself.* Sienna wondered if Jackson was happy to be apart from her. *He's been so strange lately — so secretive about his project.*

She knew it was sneaky, but Sienna decided to have a look around for Jackson's project. She opened and closed all of his drawers and cupboards carefully so he

wouldn't be able to tell that she had been there, but she couldn't find anything.

He must have taken it with him, she thought. *I can't believe he would show Luke and not me!*

That night Sienna and her parents ate pizza while they watched a DVD, which made her feel better. She loved having her

mum and dad to herself.

But after the movie all she wanted to do was go to her room. She needed to be on her own to think through all the confusing feelings she was having.

That night, Sienna had the strangest dream. She dreamt that when she looked in the mirror she saw Jackson's face instead of hers. And it made her smile.

Chapter Nine

On Sunday morning, Sienna finished off
her painting. She was really happy with
it. She rolled it up to take to school on
Monday. She didn't want anyone seeing it
until the big night!

Luke's mum dropped Jackson home
on Sunday afternoon, and Sienna went
to meet him at the front door. She was

looking forward to seeing him and thought he'd be happy to see her, too. But Jackson was acting very strangely.

'Hey, so what did you do at Luke's?' Sienna asked, following Jackson down the hall. He had his backpack in his hand.

'Um, not much,' said Jackson, not looking at Sienna.

Sienna sped up and stood at the foot of the stairs to block Jackson's way. 'You must have done something!' she insisted. 'What did you play?'

'Can you move, please?' Jackson said. 'I have to go to my room.' He pushed past Sienna to walk up the stairs, his bag still held out in front of him.

Sienna wondered if Jackson and Luke had been up to mischief. She couldn't believe he was being so mean after she'd been missing him all weekend!

'I'm talking to you!' she shouted. 'It's very rude to just ignore me.'

'Oi, you two!' their dad called from the lounge room. 'No shouting.'

But Jackson just went upstairs to his room and closed his door behind him.

What is WRONG with him? Sienna fumed. *Why is he ignoring me? We haven't seen each other all weekend!*

Sienna was about to go into her room, but then she changed her mind. She stomped all the way up to Jackson's room

and knocked loudly on the door.

'You can't come in,' Jackson called.

'Yes, I can!' Sienna growled, pushing open the door.

'That is *not* fair!' Jackson yelled, standing up quickly. His backpack was open on his bed. 'We're not allowed into each other's rooms without permission. It was *you* who made up that rule, and now *you're* the one who's breaking it! This is my room!'

Sienna felt very suspicious. 'You're hiding something!' she frowned. 'You and Luke have done something bad, haven't you?'

'It's none of your business!' Jackson shouted. 'And why would we do something

bad? You don't even *know* Luke. You don't want to talk to me anymore, and now that I've finally got my own friend, you're mean about him!'

Sienna was stunned. She hadn't meant to be mean about Luke.

Is that really what Jack thinks?

'Kids, what is all that yelling about?' their dad called from downstairs.

'Sorry, Dad,' Sienna called back. She took a deep breath and turned back to Jackson. 'What do you mean I don't want to talk to you anymore? You're the one who's always running away from me, and hiding in your room, and going to Luke's house!'

'You didn't want to hang out with me, remember?' Jackson said angrily. 'You wanted me to make my own friends. Plus *your* friends said "no boys allowed". And besides, I've been trying to talk to you all week but you never listen.'

Sienna stared at Jackson. She knew he

was right. *Some of my best friends at my last school were boys*, she realised. *Plus, my twin is a boy!*

'I'm sorry,' said Sienna, suddenly feeling awful. 'You're right. I thought you didn't want to hang out with me now that you have Luke. And I've missed you – it was so boring this weekend without you here.'

Jackson gave her a little smile. 'Really? I missed you, too. I was worried I'd have a bad dream and you wouldn't be there to make me feel better.'

'Sorry, little bro,' Sienna smiled, roughing up his hair. 'Maybe you should have told Luke to invite me, too.'

Jackson poked out his tongue.

'Hey, why don't we sleep in the same room tonight, like we used to?' Sienna said. 'You can put your mattress on my floor. In fact,' she added excitedly, 'it's been ages since we had a midnight feast.'

'Oh, I'm not sure,' Jackson said, shaking his head.

Sienna frowned, feeling confused.

But then Jackson's face broke into a grin. 'There's no way we'll fit a mattress in your room – there's too much mess! Let's do it in my room instead.'

Chapter Ten

It was Monday night and Sienna was getting ready for the art show. She sat in her room in her jeans and dressing gown, deciding which top to wear. On the left was the sparkly pink T-shirt that her mum had bought her. Pink suited Sienna, but most importantly she knew she'd match Chloe and Steph.

On the right lay her favourite T-shirt. It was the one her mum had painted for her. It had the picture of Frida Kahlo on it. She used to wear it all the time at her old school. *I wonder what Chloe and Steph would think if I wore a T-shirt with a portrait of an artist on it?* Sienna thought. *Especially a funny-looking artist with big bushy eyebrows.*

Eventually, Sienna pulled on the pink T-shirt. Then she wandered into Jackson's room to see what he was wearing. To her dismay, Jackson was wearing his favourite bright yellow T-shirt.

Sienna pulled a face as she sat on the edge of his bed, watching him fix his sticky-up hair. 'You're wearing that T-shirt?' she

said eventually, fiddling with the bracelet around her wrist.

'Yeah, I thought I'd wear my lucky T-shirt because it's a special night,' Jackson said, trying to smooth down some of the worst bits of his hair with spit. 'It would be great if the exhibition earned enough money to buy the water tank, wouldn't it?'

Sienna sighed, not really listening. She was wondering what Chloe and Steph might say about Jackson's daggy top. She fiddled with her bracelet some more. 'You know what, Jack? Yellow's not such a great colour on redheads.'

'Really?' Jackson said, peering into the mirror.

'It's just that, you know, with our red hair and pale skin … well, all those bright colours together are fine for painting, but not really for wearing.'

'Oh,' Jackson said, nodding intently. He began to take off his T-shirt.

Suddenly Sienna felt bad. *It's time you stopped telling Jack what to do*, she told herself. *So what if he wants to wear that awful top. It really is none of my business.*

She sat up straight and said, 'Actually, Jack, you should wear it. We just have different taste, that's all!'

'Really?' Jackson said, looking at himself in the mirror again. 'Well, it *is* my lucky T-shirt …'

Sienna laughed. 'You know what? You're so daggy that you're cool!'

Jackson gave her a strange smile. 'I don't care if I'm cool or not, really,' he said. 'I'd rather my friends think I'm funny than cool. To be funny, you just have to be yourself.'

Sienna stared at Jackson, amazed. *He's right again! What have I been thinking?* All this time she'd been so worried about fitting in with her new friends – and completely forgotten what she liked! *And it's taken my daggy little brother to point it out.*

Sienna jumped off the bed and gave Jackson a huge hug. 'You're the best!' she said, ruffling his hair.

'Hey!' he said. 'You're messing it up!'

'Wear it messy!' Sienna said over her shoulder, striding out of Jackson's bedroom. 'It makes you look like *you*!' Then she went to her bedroom to change.

Jackson, Sienna and their mum and dad pulled into the school car park. They were running late as usual and the car park was almost full.

'Looks like a good turnout,' their dad said, as he drove slowly around the grounds, looking for a park. 'Might get that water tank, kids!'

'You two are suspiciously quiet,' their mum said, twisting around in the front seat to look at them. 'You're not fighting, are you?'

Sienna grabbed Jackson's hand and

squeezed it. He smiled at her. Sienna was so excited and she could tell he felt the same. That was the great thing about being twins.

The school hall looked amazing. The walls were lined with everyone's artwork, and there were people everywhere. Sienna and Jackson each grabbed a plastic cup of cordial from the trestle table in the foyer.

'Hey, there's Mr Paul!' Jackson said. 'Let's go and say hi.'

They made their way through the crowd to meet Jackson's teacher. Mr Paul was holding a plate of biscuits in one hand. He shook their parents' hands vigorously with the other. 'Great to meet you, Mr and Mrs

Hartford,' Mr Paul said. 'Jackson's a great kid. He's quite a joker! And obviously very artistic, too. The sign that he and Luke made is fantastic. Where does he get his artistic talent?'

Their dad raised his eyebrows and turned to look at Jackson, who was blushing red. 'I'm afraid that's their mother's talent,' he said, smiling.

Their mum laughed as she put her arm around their dad. 'It's true — their dad doesn't have an artistic bone in his body. But he's great at maths!'

'Well, that must be where Sienna gets her talent from,' Mr Paul said, smiling at Sienna. 'Ms Diamond has been telling me

how good your maths is.'

Sienna felt her cheeks heat up and a smile stretch right across her face.

'Oh, there's the principal calling us inside,' Mr Paul said. 'The auction part of the art show will be starting soon.'

'Quick, let's go inside and get good seats,' Sienna said.

'But we haven't even seen your artwork yet,' her mum complained.

'It doesn't matter, Mum. They're going to show all the paintings at the auction,' Sienna said. 'Oh, there's Steph and Chloe!'

The two girls weaved through the crowd towards Sienna, giggling and waving. Then they stopped and stared at Sienna's T-shirt.

Uh-oh, Sienna thought, a little bit worried. *They're both wearing pink sparkly T-shirts like they said they would.*

But Steph just grinned at her and said, 'Hey, cool T-shirt!'

'Yeah,' agreed Chloe. 'Is she that Spanish painter?'

'Um, yes,' Sienna said, surprised. 'It's Frida Kahlo.'

Suddenly, it occurred to Sienna that Steph and Chloe liked her even though she was different. *In fact*, she realised, *they like me BECAUSE I'm different to them. I've been worrying about nothing all this time. Maybe people can be different to each other and still be friends. Just like Jackson and me.*

'You can go and sit with your friends, if you like,' Sienna's mum said in her ear.

'Nah,' Sienna replied. 'I think I'll sit next to Jack tonight.' She smiled at Chloe and Steph. 'I hope you don't mind.'

'No problem. We'll see you after,' Steph said. Chloe waved and the girls walked off.

Sienna didn't need to look at Jackson to know that he was smiling his big goofy smile.

go girl

flip it!

Flip to Jackson's Side...

...if you haven't read it yet!

go girl

flip it!

Secret
Chapter!

Only open after you've
read both sides of the story.

Once you've read both sides, cut open carefully along the line to read the secret chapter!

Even though the school hall was very full, Jackson, Sienna and their parents managed to find good seats not too far from the front. The twins sat next to each other, with their mum and dad on either side of them.

Both Jackson and Sienna were buzzing with excitement. It had been such a big few weeks at their new school, especially with this amazing art show! The fact that neither of them knew what the other had painted somehow made it feel even more special.

Normally, they told each other everything. But things had been so different since they moved house.

Sienna squeezed Jackson's hand as the lights went out. 'I hope you like my painting,' Sienna whispered.

'I hope you like *my* painting!' Jackson whispered back.

Mr Stevens, the music teacher, walked up on stage and stood in front of the audience. He waited for everyone to quieten down.

'This is so exciting,' said Sienna, nudging Jackson.

'And it was all our idea,' Jackson reminded her.

'I know we've had a few fights recently, but we are the best twins ever,' Sienna said to Jackson.

She could see his smile even though it was dark.

'Definitely!' Jackson whispered. 'Oops, Mr Stevens is talking. Shh ...'

Mr Stevens introduced himself and congratulated the staff and students involved in the auction. 'And I would especially like to thank the Hartford twins for coming up with such a great fundraising idea in the first place!'

Sienna and Jackson grinned at each other.

'Let's hope we can get that water tank!' continued Mr Stevens. 'Now, as you know, the theme for tonight's portrait exhibition is *Who Inspires You*?

Let's look at the first portrait for sale tonight. Here is a beautiful painting by Sophie Bennett. Sophie says her grandpa is her hero. She's painted him wearing his war medals. Isn't it great! Who would like to start the bids?'

Lots of people put up their hands and Sophie's painting sold quickly. Then the next painting sold and the next one and the one after that. Mr Stevens worked his way through the list. People bid on every painting.

Even though most paintings weren't expensive, there were loads of them. Sienna's maths brain was ticking over like a cash register. She was sure they

were close to their target to buy the water tank.

Luke's dad and Mr Paul both bid on Luke's painting. Sienna and Jackson watched as each man called out a higher number than the one before. Finally Mr Paul shook his head, smiling. He called out to Luke's dad, 'OK, you can have it.'

Chloe's portrait was bought by Ms Diamond. But neither Jackson nor Sienna's work had come up on display.

Sienna started to feel nervous. Jackson was fidgeting, like he always did when he was worried about something. They both wondered whether they were going to be last.

What if everyone had run out of money by the time theirs came up? Especially because their mum had already bought three paintings! Some people with tired toddlers or cranky babies were starting to leave.

Finally, just when Jackson and Sienna felt like they were going to burst, Mr Stevens called the hall back to attention. It had started to get pretty noisy with all of the restless kids and chatty parents.

'First of all,' Mr Stevens began, 'we've done a quick tally and I am thrilled to say that we have already reached our target! We've got enough money to buy the school a water tank!'

Everyone in the room cheered and clapped. Sienna and Jackson were pleased about the water tank, but they still felt worried. What about *their* portraits?

'Maybe they lost them?' Jackson whispered, sounding worried.

'I hope not,' Sienna said, biting her lip.

Then Mr Stevens spoke into the microphone again. 'I have kept two portraits until the end, and you'll see why in a minute.'

The hall went quiet again. Sienna gripped Jackson's hand. Then, not one but two paintings were brought onto the stage. Sienna and Jackson stared at their

artwork in amazement. The paintings were almost identical!

'Obviously, the Hartford twins worked very closely together to create these wonderful portraits of each other,' Mr Stevens said, grinning at the twins. 'In fact, other than the hair, it's hard to tell which is which, isn't it? So, I've decided to sell them as a pair – and I'll certainly be putting in a bid myself!'

Jackson and Sienna stared at the portraits, then at each other. Each had painted the other as the person who inspired them the most!

'They're beautiful, darlings!' their mum said excitedly, putting up her hand

to bid. 'But I thought you said you'd kept the portraits secret from each other?'

'We did!' said the twins at the same time.

Sienna and Jackson knew just then that they were thinking exactly the same thing. It was great to be a twin!